ADVENTURES OF
ROOP
THE SECRET RIDE ON GROXY

Dr Harmeet Kaur Bhalla

First published in 2022 by

BecomeShakespeare.com

One Point Six Technologies Pvt. Ltd.

119-123, 1st floor, Building No. J2, Wadala East,

Wadala Truck Terminal, Mumbai, Maharashtra 400037, India

T: +91 8080226699

Copyright © 2022

ISBN: 978-93-5610-957-5

CONTENTS

Happy Birthday!

CHAPTER ONE

On the hilltop in the beautiful tea gardens of Darjeeling lived a charming girl Roop. From her windows, she could touch the clouds. She often wondered what lay behind the clouds. She stayed in a big house with her parents, grandmother and grandfather. Roop was eight years old. She loved to play with her dolls.

Roop was born in a family of doctors. Mr Amit Paul and Mrs Shelly Paul were doctors in the nearby village government hospital. Her grandfather Mr Anil Paul and grandmother Mrs Rini Paul too were doctors.

Roop's parents stayed in the village of Champa. Every Friday they came to the city. Her grandma and grandpa loved her. She studied in Grade three at St. Mary's School. They sent her to school every day. Her grandfather went to the bus stop with her every morning at 8.00 A.M. and 3 P.M to send her and pick her from the bus stop.

It was the 15th of September and Roop's birthday. Since she had understood the meaning of happy birthday, she waited for this day every year. Every year she got a special gift from her parents.

That day too she woke up in the morning with the alarm.

Roop ran to her grandmother, hugged her tightly and said, "Good morning dadi…. I am so happy…. today I want something special in tiffin."

Her grandmother said, "Of course, darling today, I have prepared sandwiches for you…you like cheese sandwiches……and french fries…. I have packed your tiffin."

"You are such a sweet dadi," said Roop cuddling her grandmother.

She was eight years old now. It was a weekday and her parents decided to come in the evening. She knew this well so she quickly dressed in a beautiful blue frock for school. Her mother had specially bought it for her from the biggest kids shop in the mall.

Roop carried a box of chocolates for her friends too. Her grandfather held the chocolates and carefully took her to the bus stop as it was her birthday. She carefully got on the bus as she did not want to spoil her dress.

In school, her class teacher Mrs Paul wished her 'Happy Birthday' and patted her cheek. Roop was very excited and her friends gathered around her.

When the bell for the second period rang her class teacher made all the children sing the happy birthday song. She distributed chocolates to all her classmates and teachers. Roop was very happy.

When she reached home in the afternoon, she was surprised to see the living room decorated with colourful balloons for the evening party. Her mother took her to her room and showed her another beautiful silver dress. In one corner on her study table lay a huge gift pack.

Roop asked her mother, "Whose gift is this mom? Is this mine?"

Her mother said softly, "It is for you Roop, your dad brought this and we will open it after your party."

All the relatives and her few friends were invited to the evening party. She blew the candles and cut the pretty blue cake. She had told her mother that she wanted a mermaid cake. All her friends wore caps and sang the birthday song.

She played passing the parcel and dumb charades with her friends. All her friends relished the chocolate balls, Strawberry shake, and cutlets made by her mother, and grandmother. All the people left by seven-thirty.

CHAPTER TWO

Roop got many big and small gifts but her mind was occupied with the huge gift lying in her room.

After the party, she quickly reached her room with her mom. After changing her clothes, she ran towards the table. She tried to pick up the gift but couldn't, so she called out to her mother,

"Oh my God! it is too heavy mom……please open…. please mom."

Her mother could understand her curiosity.

She said, "Yes Roop ……come and sit on your bed so that you can have a closer look."

Her father too entered the room by then and helped his mom to carry the gift to the bed. It was wrapped in pink and silver paper. She quickly settled and started rubbing her eyes. Her mother slowly opened the gift.

Roop shouted on top of her voice, "What is this mom? It's shining like diamonds....so many colours....so many balls.... I want to play with it."

"No Roop.... I will explain how to play with it.... you cannot play just now."

She was not ready to listen and her mother noticed tears in her eyes.

"Okay Roop don't cry my child I know your excitement."

Roop started touching her gift with her gentle hands, "Mom ...these small switches....so tiny."

"You will see the magic when you switch them on.... they will brighten up your room. If you place your hand on the right planet it will lighten up."

Roop embraced her mother lovingly and said, "Mummy please start it.... please.... I can't wait till morning."

Shelly and Amit loved their only daughter. She was an apple of their eye. They carefully carried it to the table. Amit took the wire and plugged it carefully. He switched off all the other lights so that Roop could see the lights. He slowly placed his hands on the switch and in the meantime, her mother covered her eyes with her palms.

As he switched it on gentle music started playing and she gently removed her palms.

Roop was wonderstruck on seeing the scintillating lights in the room. The ceiling of the

room looked like the sky with stars twinkling all around.

She started clapping and shouted, "Mom and dad all these lights are amazing…… these balls are rotating…. all in different shapes…. beautiful."

"What do these coloured balls mean?" asked Roop.

"You see the sky every day at night. Have you noticed the millions of twinkling stars? Some shine brighter than others. Space has planets too. I will discuss this later. Now you can just sit and count them. They are eight in all."

"Eight planets….and these rings around it. What are they?"

"Now you go off to sleep as you have to go to school in the morning. I will switch off the light."

"Mom please let the lights of this gift be on…. please don't switch it off."

"Okay, you can keep watching it…. I will switch it off when you go off to sleep."

She hugged her mother and said, "Thank you mom and pa…. thank you…. good night."

She wanted them to leave early so that she could sit and have a closer look. Her parents closed the door slowly and left.

Roop's excitement knew no bounds and she jumped to sit on the table to see her gift.

The mesmerising lights emerged from all the planets. In one corner was the huge glowing hot sun. She tried to touch it but was surprised to feel the warmth on her palms.

The moon seemed to be quite cool.

She saw a strange object with two toys shaped like humans near it in one corner. She was tired so she got down from the table and moved towards her bed. She fell off to sleep as she lay on the bed.

CHAPTER THREE

Roop woke up with a strange sound when it was almost midnight. She rubbed her eyes and was shocked to see the two toys placed on the game growing bigger. They soon jumped down with a thud. She was frightened and ran to hide behind the curtains. They had coloured lights on their bodies. The two of them were laughing in their squeaky voice.

They called out in a thin voice, "Roop…. Roop……come…. come."

"No…. please go…. Go," she screamed. She caught hold of the curtain.

"Who are you? I don't know you. How can I go with a stranger? Mom and dad told me not to go with strangers. How did you become big? You were so small," said Roop.

"We are your friends, not strangers. We belong to another planet. We have been punished and sent on earth."

Roop tried to gather courage. She felt inconvenient with them as they resembled the strange creatures she had seen on television.

"I have seen you on television.... you are the same.... Tippy and Sippy."

The short one answered, "No, we are Dimdim and Kimkim."

Roop stood with her hands on her waist and asked, "Who is Dimdim?"

The short one out of the two raised his hand slowly and said, "I am Dimdim and my brother Kimkim is taller than me. Rest all the things are similar. Please join us.... we will have fun.... believe in us."

"We will take you to a mysterious ride on Groxy... you will have a ride. You will see a new world.... The exoplanet...full of precious stones.... coloured ones.... you can play with them for hours...you will enjoy it."

"No, I can't leave my mom...pa."

"You will come back in three hours," spoke the green coloured one.

The curiosity was arising in her slowly. Still holding the curtain, she asked inquisitively, "You were telling me a name.... I forgot.

"O! you are talking about the tree Groxy."

"What is Groxy? How will we go?"

She straightened her pink night suit and moved further to shake hands. She again stood at a certain distance from them.

"Come…come," they called her again.

"How will we go?" Roop asked them again.

"See outside…. see the space tree…. outside your window…. you can hear the sound," said Dimdim pointing his finger towards the glass window.

Roop ran towards the window to see the huge tree with colourful fruits flying in the air outside the window. She opened the window and tried to touch the branches but they were a bit far.

"Dimdim…Kimkim…. come…. how can we go on a tree……I will fall? Why has a tree come to take us?"

"Roop…. many trees called Groxy come every day……to give pure air to earth……people will die if they inhale poisonous air."

Roop asked still trying to catch hold of the leaves, "From where? Is there a new world……. one more earth?"

"Yes, you will enjoy once you enter……this is the biggest tree and we travel on it…let us go…. we can't wait till morning…. the tree will disappear," shouted Dimdim.

All of them moved towards the window and climbed on the window sill. Roop noticed the tree moving towards them. They easily climbed on the branch and moved towards the small hut in the middle.

Roop opened her mouth with surprise, "Wow this is so beautiful…. a tiny treehouse with a chair, a kitchen and a washroom. It looks like a dream house."

She started running in the house, "O Dimdim… Kimkim…I love this house…It is like my doll's house."

Kimkim moved towards the chair, "Roop you can sit on this chair. We will soon fly come on …let us move."

"I want to play with you…let us play hide and seek."

They almost shouted as the tree had started moving, "No once the tree moves it flies at great speed. Be careful sit down, Roop."

CHAPTER FOUR

As the tree started flying Roop started crying and shouting at the top of her voice, "Help!....Help! I will fall."

The tree was moving with great speed and she noticed the tree throwing gases outside.

Kimkim ran to give her a handkerchief, "No Roop…. you will not fall…. you are safe…. see we are sitting comfortably…. this house is a treehouse…. just hold the chair."

Now Roop gently looked outside and was happy to see a galaxy of stars shining beautifully. She had never seen the night sky so closely. She often wondered about the distance and size of the moon and stars.

Roop called out in a loud voice, "Kimkim …. Dimdim this is the real sky."

Kimkim said smiling, "Yes Roop see the way the stars shine…. they are big not small…. you can even touch them."

Roop was surprised to see the moon and she screamed, "See…Oh my God, the Moon is huge…. can we go near it?"

"No, the Moon has no air…. we live on another planet…. we will go there."

Roop asked excitingly, "What are planets? Even my mom was telling me about it."

Dimdim came to reply, "Do you know we have eight planets. I see them every day…. Mercury, Venus, Earth"

Roop stopped him by pointing out towards the open sky, "Where is Earth? What colour? I know we live on it."

"Yes, Roop the Earth is blue and green…. we live on it."

Dimdim continued, "Mercury, Venus, Earth, Mars, Jupiter…the biggest one, Saturn with rings Uranus, Neptune."

Roop opened her mouth and kept her right hand on her forehead, "So many…I can't even remember them…. such big names…there are thousands I feel…. they are special I suppose."

She noticed fruits of rainbow colours hanging from the tree. She wanted to pluck them and eat but she was locked. She knew if the doors and windows opened, she would fall. The tree had several holes in the trunk.

Roop was curious so she asked, "Dimdim can I eat these fruits? I am hungry."

"No Roop they are for us and people who do not live on the earth. You cannot eat…. don't even try."

Roop could not control herself and said, "Okay…just one blue fruit…. please…it is looking so tempting."

She kept admiring the fruits hanging and flying in the air. Her mouth started watering. The tree too was moving at a great speed. Suddenly the holes in the tree Groxy started throwing colourful gases.

Roop screamed, "Oh Dimdim…Kimkim…. such a lot of gas…. I cannot see the stars anymore…it is dark outside."

Dimdim spoke in an angry tone, "Wait and watch…. the sky will become clear…. the earth is full of polluted airs…. people from different planets are helping the earth."

"How is it possible?" asked Roop in a surprising manner.

The gas could not enter the treehouse, but she could see the sky with the stars and the moon after a few minutes. Roop was hungry now and she could only see the fruits hanging outside flying in the air.

She remembered that they had told her not to eat.

She thought, "Why are they telling not to eat it? She could easily pluck them."

She wanted to give it a try so she moved towards the window and tried to open it. The window was tightly locked. In one corner she saw a stick so she gathered courage and stood up.

She almost fell, "Oh! Oh!...I am dancing.... help"

Dimdim and Kimkim ran to help her "We told you not to move you have to sit."

Roop got the stick and stood holding the window tightly.

She told them, "I will stand here and watch the sky."

As Dimdim and Kimkim turned their face Roop started opening the window slowly. She managed to take out her hand and caught hold of the blue fruit in the shape of an orange. She tried to break it but failed to do so. She took her stick and hit it hard and finally the blue fruit was in her hand.

CHAPTER FIVE

Roop was so happy to hold it in her hand. It was a sea blue coloured fruit with purple leaves. She kept looking at it as she had never seen such a fruit. She looked around and found both of them handling the tree gas plant.

She wanted to eat it anyhow because it looked so attractive. The moment she took a bite she started laughing.

Dimdim and Kimkim ran towards her.

"What have you eaten? The Blue Tangy….my God…. What will we do?"

Roop went on giggling and soon she started turning blue.

"Oh…. Oh…I am turning blue…. I am becoming fat…. see…see."

Roop started becoming round and round like a ball. She finally became a blue ball with two eyes

stuck out. Kimkim and Dimdim kept holding her as she was rolling in the treehouse. She became a huge fat round blue ball.

She went right and left then again north and south, "Dimdim....I am enjoying my new shape.... my new colour ha...ha...ha....let me roll....ha... ha."

Dimdim almost shouted, "Roop please sit in one corner. What will I tell King Pimpim?"

Roop giggled and asked, "Oh What a funny name...... Pimpim.... ha ...ha ...Pimpim."

Kimkim said keeping both his hands on his head, "He will get angry. He had given instructions not to eat the fruit. You are full of poison now."

Roop went on tumbling and suddenly got stuck in one corner, "Why? Come and free me.... tell me how will I come back to my old self.... I can't go to my mom like this...remove this colour."

Dimdim and Kimkim caught hold of her from both sides, "You stay in one place as we are about to reach. These fruits contain all the dirty gases of the earth.... now you will have to climb the mountain of Zinzin and then take bath in the Blue Sea."

Roop became teary-eyed, "How is this possible? My body is full of infection now...I can't climb ...I can't take bath. I have become a ball now...I will roll down.... help me...please...please."

"We have to follow the rules of our king, he eats and sleeps the whole day.... let us see."

The tree kept flying for another fifteen minutes and Roop was held by the two of them. She could not cry because whoever ate the fruit would only laugh.

The tree slowed down as they were about to reach. Roop could not see the new place properly because her shape had changed.

She kept on giggling and asked, "Where am I? Dimdim…Kimkim…. Have we reached your house?"

"Yes…you are welcome to our house."

Soon she heard a loud noise and she looked outside. Groxy had taken its position as it became straight. The tree was throwing all the gases again outside.

On seeing the air turning pink in colour Roop laughed again, "Oh is the air pink in colour here…. lovely."

CHAPTER SIX

Groxy suddenly became still and the door of the treehouse started opening.

Roop opened her eyes to see the new land with precious stones lying everywhere. Red, blue, green, purple and yellow stones were scattered all around. She blinked her eyes as she was already in a very uneasy position.

She called out, "Please help…I want to return to my original self again.…I want to be free."

Dimdim and Kimkim helped her in getting down from the treehouse. It was quite difficult for them to carry a ball. They placed her on the ground carefully.

Kimkim said to Dimdim, "Let us go to our majesty King Pimpim. We have to tell him about our new guest. We have to take his permission to go to Mount Zinzin."

"Yes, let us go and meet him."

They rolled Roop towards the palace made of diamonds. The palace was sparkling and the guards did not stop them. Kimkim asked them, "Is his majesty awake? We have to take permission."

"No, he is fast asleep.... he will wake up tomorrow.... don't disturb."

"It is urgent.... please. We don't have time."

Dimdim looked at Kimkim with a sad face and said, "What will we do now.... she has to return after three hours."

Roop was listening to all this when she thought of an idea. She struggled to free herself from them. She laughed loudly and rolled all over the palace.

Dimdim and Kimkim ran to catch her, "Stop.... stop Roop" they shouted but as there was a lot of noise the king woke up.

Suddenly King Pimpim woke up from his sleep. He came running towards the ball and stopped it with his hands.

Roop was surprised to see such a tiny man wearing a gown made of purple leaves and a diamond crown.

She said while still laughing, "Who are you? Oh my God! you look so funny.... look at his tiny hands and feet.... his curly green moustache and he has no teeth."

"Roop shut your mouth…this is his majesty King Pimpim."

"What is all this? This ball has eyes…. blue ball. It speaks?"

Dimdim and Kimkim ran to catch her and bowed in front of him, "My Lord …. this ball is a girl Roop. She has come with us to see our planet."

"Who is she? How dare she laughs at me …. shut up you fool…I know she must have done a mistake like you two."

"Sorry, your majesty…. She has eaten the Blue Tangy. Please help her."

"Tell her to stop laughing at me."

Dimdim scolded her, "Roop stop…Your Majesty, please help her as she is in trouble."

"She is very naughty. Make her climb the Mountain Zinzin…as the Blue Sea is there. Jadoo will help her in taking a dip in the water."

"One more request your majesty," said Dimdim.

"We are tired of living on earth like statues. Please tell the magician Jadoo to let us return to the planet."

The King looked at them and curled his moustaches, "You have to do your duty well…. if you do not take Groxy every day it will die…. Jadoo is in his house at Mount Zinzin…. you have to say sorry to him."

He continued, "This girl is naughty.... if she keeps laughing, she will be punished like the two of you. Go quickly now as Jadoo will go to his magical hut."

The three of them said, "Yes your majesty .... yes."

They hurried out of the palace with Roop rolling out of the palace.

In front of the palace was a huge mountain with huge rocks on all sides. A small passage in one corner would lead them to the top.

"It will take one hour to reach and Roop you have to be back before five o'clock. Let us hurry.... Come on," said Dimdim and pushed Roop along with Kimkim

CHAPTER SEVEN

Dimdim and Kimkim caught her from both sides and started climbing.

Roop's body was hurting now and she shouted, "Carry me properly…I have become a ball but my body is the same."

They rolled her up carefully in between the rocks.

Dimdim sat down looking up towards the mountain still holding the ball, "Oh I am tired I still can't see Jadoo's house from here……I hope we find him there."

Kimkim replied trying to protect Roop from getting hurt, "Be careful…only three hours are left for you to return."

"She has to take a dip in the ice-cold water of the Blue Sea…. I hope she doesn't fall sick."

Roop said in a trembling voice, "Is the water cold? I always take bath with hot water."

"Come on don't waste time let's go."

Roop wanted to enjoy her trip but with her body like a ball she could not. She wanted to see Jadoo now.

"I am feeling thirsty…. I want water."

They moved towards the rock and placed her in such a way so that she did not roll down. Dimdim ran towards the water flowing down and took out a glass made of leaves. He bent down to collect water carefully.

"Drink this water…. you will find it salty."

Dimdim poured the water into her mouth. Roop shouted, "Stop…I can't drink…. stop."

Kimkim and Dimdim started their journey again.

In fifteen minutes, they reached the top of Mount Zinzin.

Dimdim and Kimkim started dancing and singing, "We have finally reached…. Roop."

Dimdim shouted, "Let us call Jadoo."

They started shouting "Jadoo…. Jadoo…. come out."

Suddenly the clouds thundered and a small man appeared.

Roop saw that he had only eyes, a small mouth on the face with his six hands and legs dancing in the air.

"Oh! .....Jadoo," screamed both of them.

Jadoo started shouting "So you are here finally. You both are careless and lazy."

Dimdim and Kimkim sat down in front of him and said, "No, we just got late…please spare us… please. We don't want to go to the earth. You have to help this girl Roop also."

Roop interfered and said, "Help me he looks so dangerous."

"Don't be afraid Roop he is Jadoo. He will help you."

Jadoo looked at her and said, "This blue ball… even she didn't obey you I think."

"Yes, she ate the Blue Tangy…. please give her a dip in the Blue Sea quickly as she has to go back."

"Roll the ball behind me," said Jadoo and moved towards the river. In ten minutes, they reached the Blue Sea.

Roop had never seen such a clearwater river. The blue colour looked very cool.

CHAPTER EIGHT

Roop was afraid to take a dip as the water was cold. She could see ice in the corners. She blinked her eyes.

Jadoo started using his magical power and spread his hands. He picked up Roop and threw her in the water.

Roop started floating in the water and she shouted "Help! Help! I don't know how to swim… Dimdim Kimkim…. I will drown."

Dimdim called out almost tumbling down in the water, "No Roop you can easily float in this water. You are safe. This sea is not deep."

The blue sea started turning dark blue and Roop disappeared for a few seconds. Jadoo kept reading the lines,

Leave the blue

Come back you

Magic has begun

Do not run

After five minutes the water had large ripples and Roop came out as a lovely girl of eight and the blue colour disappeared.

Jadoo stretched his long hands and she quickly held his hands. He pulled her out. Roop stood on the uneven mountain and was happy to look at herself.

She screamed with surprise, "See…see…I am back to the same Roop…see my hands my fingers all are back…. I am the same…. same."

Jadoo started smiling on seeing her. He had never seen human beings from the planet Earth.

Jadoo called out, "Dimdim you have brought her…. I have never seen people from the earth."

"There are boys and girls on earth…. we go every day so we know…. she is a girl."

He almost scolded her, "Why did you bring her?"

"It is because of your punishment. As you had changed us into toys. We looked like astronauts so we were placed on Roop's birthday gift."

Jadoo spoke in an angry tone, "You deserve punishment. You know we have one thousand Groxy trees and they need to go every day. If they do not go they will die as well as the people."

Kimkim spoke softly now, "But Jadoo we could not go just for one day…. please take back your punishment…. we cannot live there just like statues…. we need to come back."

"You have to promise to be punctual…. you are always late…even if one of my trees die my people too will fall ill," said Jadoo.

Both of them said together in the same tone, "Sir we promise to be obedient. Please….please."

"Okay from now onwards you will be free. If you are late again then…." said he almost growling.

Roop looked all around strangely and turned towards Jadoo, "Uncle you have so many hands…. and legs."

Suddenly Dimdim and Kimkim came forward, "Don't ask anything now. Don't waste time Roop you have only two hours left. Let us go now."

The three of them waved goodbye and started running downward.

CHAPTER NINE

They came down from Mount Zinzin in fifteen minutes as they were running fast. Roop was enjoying her visit to this exoplanet.

Roop sat down breathing heavily on the colourful ground and said, "I am thirsty……my throat is dry……give me some other water…. I will not drink salty water."

Dimdim ran to bring water from a small hut. He came out carrying water in a pipe and placed it on Roop's mouth. She gulped down the water and said, "Thank You"

Kimkim happily said, "In these one and a half hours you can roam around freely on our exoplanet."

Roop wanted to ask many questions. She saw coloured stones and Groxy everywhere. They looked very pretty. She saw so many tree houses.

Roop asked dancing all around, "Why are there so many stones? There is no sand."

Dimdim answered picking up a handful of stones and started eating them, "My planet has diamonds of different colours. We eat them whenever we feel hungry."

"What? How can you eat them?" asked Roop trying to pick them up.

Both of them rushed to stop her and took the stones from her hand, "You cannot eat them.... you will become a stone."

They snatched and threw down the stones. Roop secretly kept one blue diamond in her pocket.

Roop started dancing around the trees. She was so excited, "Oh my God! thousands of trees.... with colourful fruits. Why have you named them Groxy."

"Groxy are trees helping the people on the earth to breathe pure air. They go at night and nobody can see them."

Roop was almost yawning when she said, "We sleep peacefully...we don't even know."

Dimdim took her hand and reached the corner of the planet, "See the trees are returning now."

Roop could see thousands of Groxy flying towards them.

She opened her eyes and mouth wide and said, "How do manage it? Two of you.... Jadoo.... King Pimpim....my God"

"We keep watching the planet Earth. We have so many brothers to help us."

"Where are they? I want to meet them."

Dimdim and Kimkim said in a sad tone, "They will return soon but before that, it is time for you to go back"

Roop was about to fall when Kimkim pulled her back and said, "Be careful Roop."

Roop asked with her eyes continuously fixed on the trees that were returning and fixing themselves, "Do tell me about this strange term Groxy."

"Groxy is green plus oxygen. The earth will be green if it gets sufficient oxygen."

They held her hand and moved towards their treehouse in Groxy.

"I have not yet gone all around.... I love this place. Can I come again?" Saying this she almost cried.

They said, "We can try but don't waste time."

CHAPTER TEN

"Wake up Roop…. wake up," shouted her grandmother.

Her grandfather too was sitting next to her, "It is seven o'clock and you will miss your bus."

Roop was enjoying her sound sleep. She woke up to hear the voice of her grandparents.

She started calling out with her eyes still closed, "Dimdim…Kimkim…. Groxy."

Her grandmother got upset and held Roop's hand, "What are you saying? What is Dimdim? Have you gone crazy?"

"She must have had a dream…. maybe a bad dream," her grandfather said in a worried manner.

In the meantime, Roop sat on the bed and started looking all around.

"Where am I? I don't want to be here."

She quickly got off the bed and ran towards her gift. The gift was kept in the same place.

She started looking at the two figures. They were intact.

Roop picked them up and said, "Oh they are Dimdim and Kimkim. They cannot become statues again."

Roop ran towards the window and started calling out. "Come Groxy.... I cannot see it now. Where have they gone?

Her grandparents became upset and her grandpa said,

"I think she is not well. We will have to take her to the doctor."

Roop straightened her night suit and tried to come back to her normal self. She knew the true story behind it.

She sat on the chair and thought, "Was it a dream....no.... She remembered everything now.... the beautiful world.... the thousands of trees....the colourful stones and the blue ball."

She started looking at herself and was happy that she was no more a blue ball. She shivered at the thought of the Blue River.

Suddenly she felt something heavy in her pocket. She started fumbling her pockets. Slowly she took out the blue diamond from her pocket.

A sparkling blue diamond of another world was in her hand. Roop felt on top of the world. She didn't want her grandparents to see it.

She went up to her cupboard and opened her moneybox. She kept the blue diamond in it and locked it forever.

9 789356 109575